OCTRINA THE OCTOPUS

BY
MARY JEAN POLLARD

ILLUSTRATED BY
BETTY POLLARD

Mary Jean Pollard

To order additional copies of this book, contact:
Xlibris Corporation
1-888-795-4274
www.Xlibris.com
Orders@Xlibris.com

Dedication

To Betty, our wonderful artist,

To our precious family,

To Michael, Michelle, Jim, Dave,

Erin, David, and above all,

To Bill, my helpmate and my soulmate.

"Now, Octrina, don't cry. You have everything to be happy about.

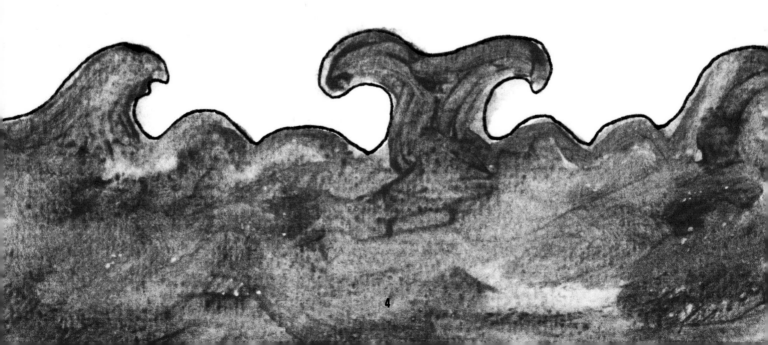

"You are a lovely little green octopus
with lots of friends."

"No, Mommy, I don't. Nobody wants to play with me."

"Yesterday when I went to the park they made me get out of the swings."

"Why, dear?"

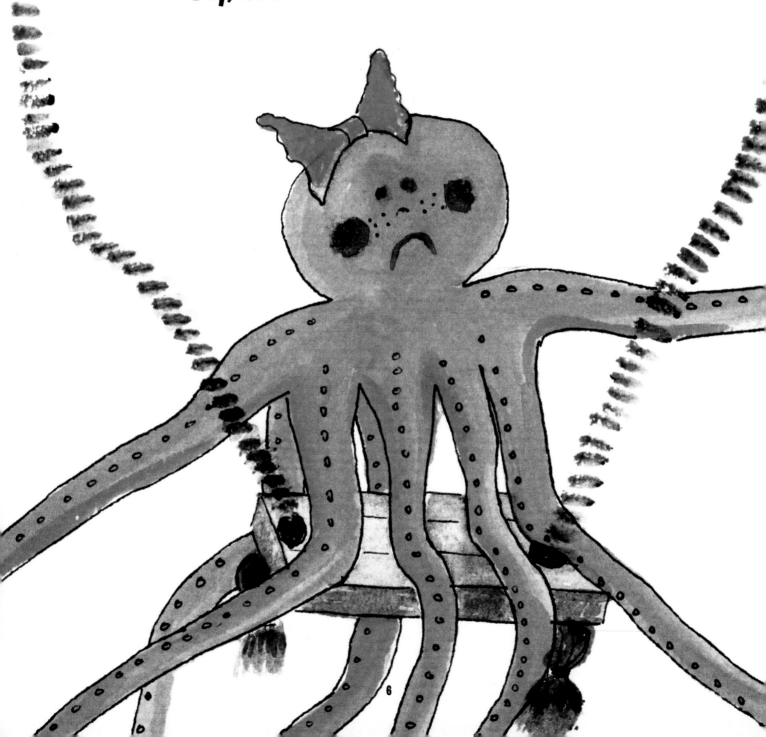

"Well, my legs stick out so bad that I knocked two children out of the swings."

"When I tried to get a box of soap and crackers at the same time at the grocery store, I pushed over a stack of soup cans.

"Mommy, what does 'Clumsy Ox' mean?"

"Now, dear, you have a beautiful smile and a lovely disposition. I'm sure you can find someone who wants to play with you."

"In spite of having eight arms."

"Well, Mommy, you know you fainted when you found out how much my school shoes would cost."

"It's all these legs - that's my problem."

"Nobody should be an octopus!"

The next day . . .

"Octrina, wake up dear. Mrs. Snapper wants you to come over and help her serve for a coffee party."

"Oh Mommy, I'll go but the last time I helped Mrs. Flounder, I broke three plates at one time."

At the end of the day Mommy was watching
out the window when Octrina came home.

"How was it, dear?"

"Well, Mother, would you believe *five?*"

"Five what , dear?

"Five plates broken!"

"Oh, dear."

Then one day while Octrina was walking along . . . doing nothing . . . and going nowhere, she saw Miss Perch run from the school building and heard her screaming.

"No, I can't be a teacher for a school of fish. You would need eight arms to teach those fish."

Octrina

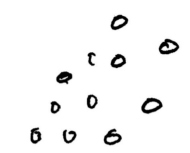

heard

just

two

words...

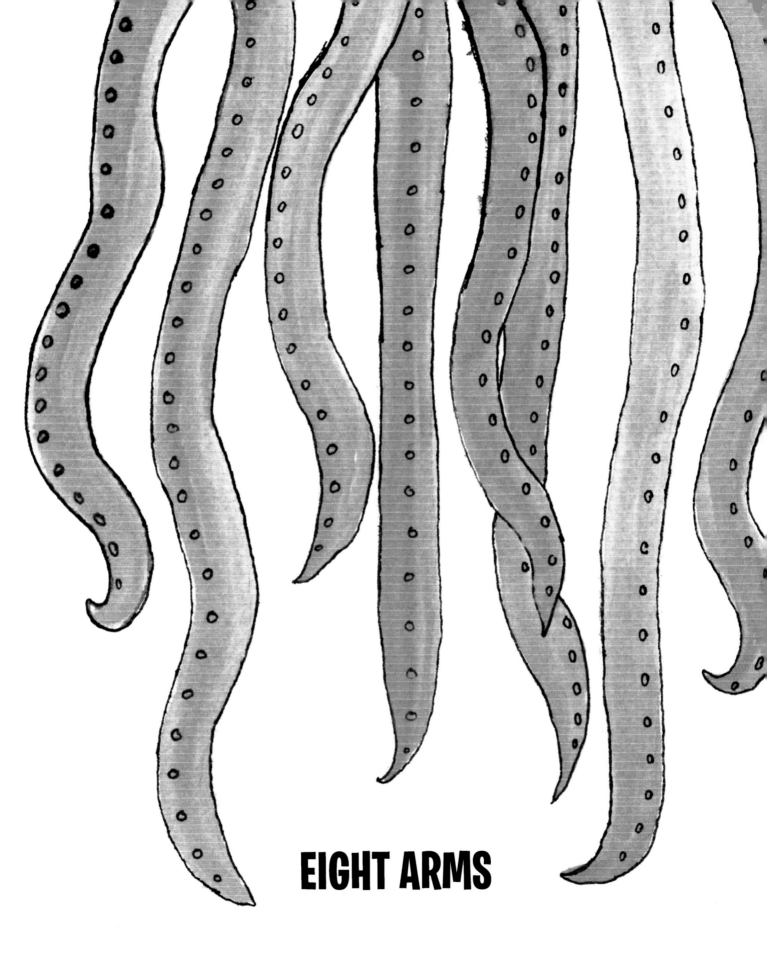

EIGHT ARMS

Octrina studied hard at teacher's college, and now Octrina is happy to be an octopus. Who else do you know who can . . .

Write on a chalkboard

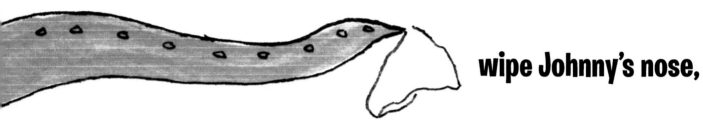

wipe Johnny's nose,

look up a word in the dictionary,

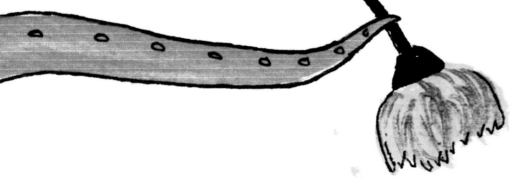

clean out her desk,

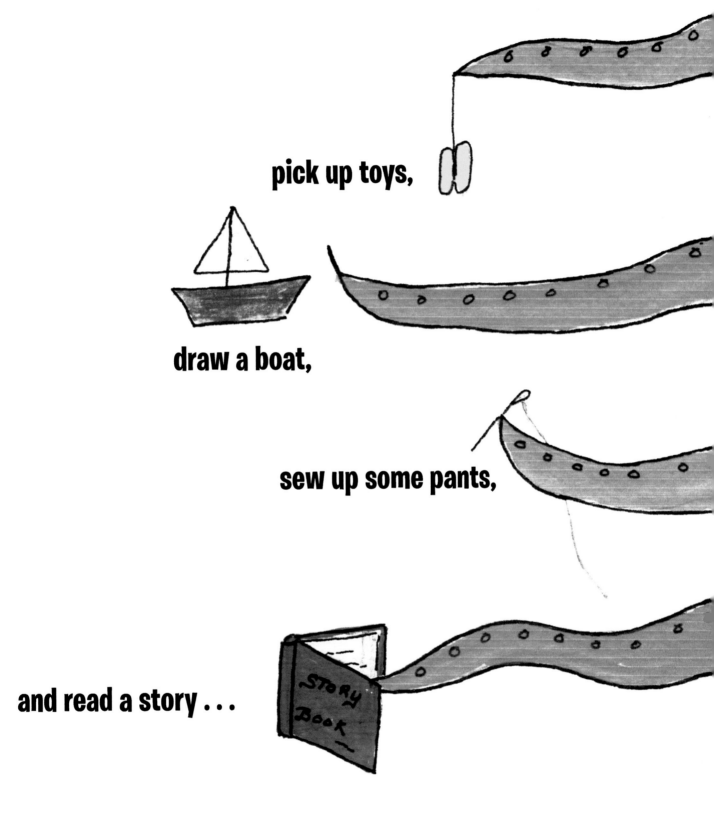

pick up toys,

draw a boat,

sew up some pants,

and read a story . . .

all at the same time?

All that time, Octrina spent worrying about what she couldn't do. She never really thought about all the things she could do.

Octrina sighed, "I'm glad to be me!"

MORAL OF THIS STORY

Do what you do best, then you will be happy.

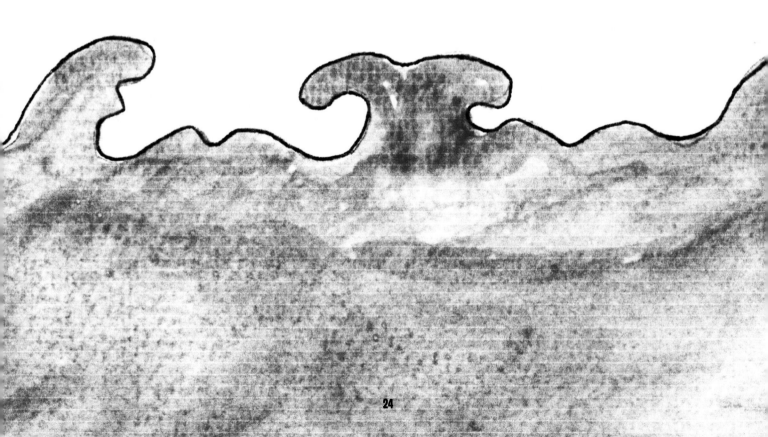

Edwards Brothers,Inc!
Thorofare, NJ 08086
01 February, 2011
BA2011032